Super Surprise

ZIGZAG KIDS

PATRICIA REILLY GIFF

Super Surprise

illustrated by

ALASDAIR BRIGHT

WENDY
LAMB
BOOKS

Text copyright © 2012 by Patricia Reilly Giff
Jacket art and interior illustrations copyright © 2012 by Alasdair Bright

Wendy Lamb Books and the colophon are trademarks
of Random House, Inc.

Visit us on the Web! randomhouse.com/kids
Educators and librarians, for a variety of teaching tools, visit us at
randomhouse.com/teachers

Library of Congress Cataloging-in-Publication Data
Giff, Patricia Reilly.
Super surprise / by Patricia Reilly Giff ;
illustrated by Alasdair Bright. — 1st ed.
p. cm.
Summary: When Destiny Washington gets the notion that everyone's
favorite teacher, Ms. Katz, is going to be dismissed from the
Zigzag Afternoon Center, she and classmate Yolanda
think of several ways to save her.
ISBN 978-0-385-73890-3 (trade) — ISBN 978-0-385-90757-6 (lib. bdg.) —
ISBN 978-0-375-89640-8 (ebook) — ISBN 978-0-375-85914-4 (pbk.)
[1. Schools—Fiction. 2. Problem solving—Fiction.]
I. Bright, Alasdair, ill. II. Title.
PZ7.G3626Str 2012
[Fic]—dc22
2011034342

Printed in the United States of America
10 9 8 7 6 5 4 3 2 1
First Edition

For Anne Reilly Eisele,
my sister,
with love
—P.R.G.

• • •

To Joe, Charlotte, Paul, and Clare
—A.B.

Yolanda

Sumiko

Charlie

Destiny

Gina

Mitchell

Habib

Clifton

Trevor

Beebe

Angel

Peter

CHAPTER 1

FRIDAY

Destiny Washington raced along the hall. She was on her way to the school library. It was movie time at the Zigzag Afternoon Center. And after that, Ms. Katz, her favorite teacher, had promised a surprise.

But wait.

A sign was tacked up on the wall.

Destiny squinted at the sign. Too bad she wasn't such a great reader.

"Rrrrrrr . . . ," she whispered.

Rhinoceros?

No good.

That animal wouldn't even fit in the school.

She stood on one foot. "That *R* word is one tough baby," she said.

Gina came up behind her. "Are you talking to yourself?"

Destiny crossed her fingers. "Just humming."

Gina pointed to the sign. "I'm going to join right in."

"Me too," Destiny said.

Hmmm. Join in what? she wondered.

Gina kept going down the hall.

"Rrrrr . . ." Destiny spelled it out: *"R-H-Y-M-E."*

And then she had it. She really did!

Rainbow!

She couldn't believe it. She'd sounded out one of the hardest words in the world.

That was it. They'd all be rainbows next week!

She'd wear her best butterfly bow. It was red and green and orange, her favorite color.

But she had to hurry. The movie would begin any minute.

She rushed down the hall.

She circled Jake the Sweeper. He was peering into the mop closet.

His face was red. "What a mess in here," he said.

Poor Jake.

Destiny was the last one in the library.

A thousand books covered the shelves. All the seats were taken. There was almost no room.

Her friend Beebe was squashed up in front. Beebe wore round aids in her ears to help her hear.

Sometimes she could even read lips!

In back, Yolanda was sitting on a bench. She moved over to make room for Destiny.

"Thanks!" Destiny slung her backpack underneath the bench.

Ms. Katz smiled at them.

"You're so lucky, Destiny," Yolanda said. "Ms. Katz is your classroom teacher. And she's the librarian for the Afternoon Center, too."

Destiny nodded. Ms. Katz was the best teacher in the school. Maybe in the whole United States of America.

The movie began. It was about a princess and a witch who locked her in a castle.

"That's what witches always do," Yolanda said.

Destiny tried to see.

The other kids' heads bobbed up and down in front of her.

Along came a godmother. She said:

I'll get you out.
Don't you worry.
I'll think of something
In a hurry.

And that was what happened.
The godmother said:

Hop in bed.
Say good night.
Hold on tight!

The princess and the bed flew out the window. They landed in a river. They sailed away.
Free.

The movie was over. Everyone clapped.

Mitchell whistled. Almost whistled. It was more of a *shu-shu* sound. He was still working on it.

Ms. Katz snapped up the shades. "Here comes the surprise. Think about the movie. What does it have to do with the sign?"

Rainbows, Destiny thought. *Colors!*

The princess wore a pink and purple gown.

Yes, that was it.

Outside the library, Destiny saw Jake go by. He was shaking his head.

Mrs. Terrible Thomas, Jake's cat, went by, too. She wasn't supposed to come to school. But she liked to sneak in.

Now Destiny was ready for the surprise.

What could it be?

CHAPTER 2

STILL FRIDAY

Ms. Katz sat on the edge of the desk. "Whew. Not an inch of room in here."

She looked around. "Can anyone guess what the surprise is?"

Destiny raised her hand. She waved it hard.

Ms. Katz looked over her eyeglasses. "Yes, Destiny?"

Destiny stood up. This news was important. Let everyone get a good look at her.

"We are going to be rainbows at the Zigzag Center next week." She twirled around.

Everyone looked surprised.

Gina covered her mouth.

Destiny could see she was trying not to laugh.

Something was wrong.

Very wrong.

Gina stood up, even though Ms. Katz hadn't called on her.

"Next week is rhyme time," Gina said. "We're going to be poets, right?"

"Yes, that's the surprise," Ms. Katz said. "You're an excellent thinker, Gina."

Destiny took a quick look at Ms. Katz.

Was Ms. Katz disappointed in her?

Destiny put her head down.

Rhyme time, not rainbow time.

She wondered if she might cry.

Probably.

Next to her, Yolanda whispered, "Don't worry. Everyone makes mistakes."

Ms. Katz was still talking. "Bring in your poems on Monday. Bring one every day next week, if you like."

Peter Petway, a sixth grader, stood up. "I'll copy some of the poems into my newspaper, *Zigzag News—Read All About It.*"

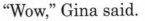

"Wow," Gina said.

Mitchell almost whistled.

Destiny swallowed. She'd never get her name in the *Zigzag News.*

She was not an excellent thinker. She wasn't even a so-so thinker.

Outside, Ramón, the college student who helped out, blew his whistle. Afternoon Center was over for the day.

Everyone scrambled for the buses.

Everyone except Destiny. She didn't scramble. She didn't want to see anyone. She didn't want anyone to see her, either.

Halfway down the hall, she remembered something.

She'd left her backpack under the bench in the library.

She had to get it. Even if she missed Bus Thirteen.

Even if she had to walk two million blocks to get home.

The backpack had her homework. Her left-over cookie from lunch. It also had last week's *Zigzag News—Read All About It*.

She rushed back to the library.

The door was still open.

Jake the Sweeper went by, pushing a broom. "No room," he was saying to himself.

Jake was right about that, Destiny thought. Books and papers were all over the place. Computers and boxes were lined up against the wall.

Jake went into the mop closet.

He was still talking to himself. "What a mess! It's really time . . ."

A bucket banged into the wall. ". . . Katz to go."

Destiny stepped around Mrs. Terrible
Thomas. She stopped on one foot.

Was Jake saying Ms. Katz had to go?

This was the worst news Destiny had ever
heard in her life.

She grabbed her backpack.

She raced outside.

Bus Thirteen was still there. It sounded as if
it were coughing.

Destiny climbed up. She sat on the ripped seat. It was the only one left.

But who cared about that?

All she could think about was Ms. Katz leaving the Zigzag Afternoon Center.

Then she thought about the godmother in the movie. The godmother who had saved the princess.

Destiny had to be like the godmother.

She had to save Ms. Katz!

CHAPTER 3

MONDAY

It was time for Afternoon Center. Destiny hurried down the stairs.

She was the lunch lady's helper. She was going to give out snacks.

She passed Ms. Katz in the hall.

Ms. Katz had a pile of papers in her arms.

She dropped them all over the place.

Destiny looked around. She hoped Jake didn't see the mess Ms. Katz had made.

She helped Ms. Katz pick up the papers. Every single scrap. Homework sheets. Drawings. Even Ms. Katz's Stop & Shop list.

Ms. Katz put her hand on Destiny's shoulder. "What would I do without you?"

Destiny smiled a little. But what would everyone do without Ms. Katz?

She looked around. Whew! Jake was nowhere in sight.

But there was Mrs. Terrible Thomas, the cat. She padded down the hall. She had sneaked into school again.

She was carrying one of her kittens.

It was the one who looked like an orange ice pop.

The cutest one.

"That one's my favorite," Destiny said.

"I think I like the gray one," said Ms. Katz. She waved and went up the stairs.

Destiny went the other way, into the lunchroom.

She wished she knew where Yolanda was.

She had to tell someone the bad news about Ms. Katz.

She needed help. Somehow, they had to save Ms. Katz.

But Yolanda wasn't in the lunchroom yet.

Destiny handed out cups of chocolate pudding. They had little whipped cream hats.

She gave a nice fat one to Gina.

"Mmmm," Gina said.

She gave two huge ones to Mitchell and Charlie.

"Thanks," Charlie said.

Mitchell almost whistled. *Shu-shu.*

Clifton, a kindergarten kid, came next.

Destiny gave him a pudding with a great swirly hat.

"This stuff is wiggly," Clifton said. He scooped the top into his mouth.

At last Yolanda came in the door.

She raced up to Destiny. "I almost didn't make it. I was working on a poem."

"I have to tell you . . . ," Destiny began.

Yolanda sank into a chair. "Do you know what rhymes with *rose*?"

Destiny thought for a moment. *"Nose,"* she said.

Yolanda slapped her forehead. "That's terrific. All I could think of was *boze* and *goze*."

Destiny was surprised at herself. *Nose.* Not bad.

"I'm a better artist than a poet." Yolanda leaned forward. "What's under that whipped cream?"

Destiny held out the pudding cup. Clifton was right. The whole thing was jiggly.

It made her laugh.

Yolanda laughed, too.

Somehow, Destiny jiggled too hard. The cup tipped. The whipped cream slid off the top.

So did a blob of chocolate pudding.

They flew onto Yolanda's shirt.

"Oh, no!" Destiny said.

Yolanda looked down at her shirt. "That's a surprise," she said, and gulped.

Destiny picked up a napkin. At least she could wipe off the mess.

That made it worse.

She felt tears coming.

"Don't worry." Yolanda headed out the door.

Destiny could see that she was trying to smile.

"Wait," Destiny called. "I have to talk to you about something."

But Yolanda disappeared down the hall.

Destiny gave out another bunch of chocolate puddings.

Sometimes she gave out two.

She had to hurry.

She had to find Yolanda.

CHAPTER 4

STILL MONDAY

First Destiny tried the library.

Ms. Katz was alone in there. She was sitting at her desk.

Books were piled up in front of her.

Destiny called hello. She kept going.

She tried the girls' room next.

Mitchell's sister, Angel, was pinning a clip in her hair.

"How do you think this looks?" Angel tilted her head.

"Neat!" Destiny said. "Do you know where—"

Angel was still talking. "I'm making up a poem about it. Listen. . . ."

Destiny wanted to hurry away. But she couldn't hurt Angel's feelings.

Angel looked up at the ceiling. *"My clip is green. I look like a . . ."* She frowned. "I don't know the rest."

"Queen," said Destiny.

"Great!" Angel said.

"Thanks." Destiny ducked out of the girls' room. She headed for the gym.

Yolanda wasn't there, either.

Sumiko was swinging on a rope. She was the best rope swinger in the school.

Where else could Destiny look?

How about outside in the school yard?

Destiny raced up the stairs. She went out the door.

Ramón was playing ball with Peter Petway and a couple of other sixth graders.

Peter's brother, Trevor, a kindergarten kid, was bashing a ball against the wall.

And there was Yolanda!

She was sitting on the cement. In front of her was a big cardboard box.

"Whew," Destiny said. "I thought I'd never find you."

"Don't worry about my shirt," Yolanda said. "I think the pudding will come out in the wash."

Destiny put her hand over her mouth. She'd forgotten about the shirt.

"I'm really sorry," she said.

She looked down into the box.

Mrs. Terrible Thomas's six kittens were rolling around. They were playing with each other. Their tiny claws were out.

Two were gray and white striped. Another two were white with black spots. One was gray, Ms. Katz's favorite.

And then there was the orange ice pop kitten.

"Orange is my favorite color," Destiny told Yolanda.

If she had a cat, she'd name it . . .

What?

Never mind what.

She had a bunch of fish in a tank. Mom said fourteen fish were enough pets in one house.

Fish didn't do very much, though. They just swam back and forth. They gulped in water.

You couldn't even tell them apart.

But never mind the fish.

It was Ms. Katz she had to think about.

"I have terrible news," she told Yolanda. "Jake says Ms. Katz has to go."

Yolanda looked as if she might cry. "Ms. Katz is the best teacher in the United States of America."

"I guess she's a little messy," Destiny said.

"We have to save her," Yolanda said.

"I know it," Destiny said.

If only she were an excellent thinker!

For a moment, they petted the kittens.

"The Afternoon Center won't be the same without Ms. Katz," Yolanda said.

"I won't have a teacher, either," Destiny said.

"How about this?" Yolanda said.

At the same time, Destiny said, "I have an idea."

"You first," Yolanda said.

Destiny nodded. "When we go home tonight, we'll think and think."

"Yes! That's what I was going to say," Yolanda told her.

They gave each other a high five.

"And somehow," Destiny said, "we'll save Ms. Katz."

CHAPTER 5

STILL MONDAY

A few minutes later, Ramón blew his whistle.

Afternoon Center was over for the day.

Destiny gave Orange Ice one last pat. If only she could take her home!

Destiny waved goodbye to Yolanda.

Yolanda was lucky. She was a walker. She'd be home in two minutes.

Destiny hurried to the gate.

She climbed onto Bus Thirteen. She sat in front next to Charlie.

The bus started up.

It was rocking back and forth.

"Here we go," Charlie said.

Bus Thirteen coughed out onto the street.

Just then—

Screeeeech!

Uh-oh.

What a horrible noise.

Destiny put her hands over her ears.

Clunk!

A puff of smoke!

Bus Thirteen slid to a stop. The smoke drifted away.

The bus driver shook her head. "This is the end of Bus Thirteen."

"I knew it," Charlie said. "It's a real clunker."

"We'll wait for another bus to come along," the driver said.

They all piled out and sat on Mr. Oakley's

front lawn. Mr. Oakley was the grandfather who helped out at the Center.

He came out and gave them pears from his tree.

Destiny chomped down on hers while they waited.

It was a long wait.

"We could make up a great poem about the bus," Charlie said. "Too bad I'm not such a great rhymer. I'm a better inventor."

A poem popped into Destiny's head.

*"Thirteen was the worst bus I ever saw.
How sad. It is no more!"*

She thought about it. "It almost rhymes," she told Charlie.

"It's a super poem." He grinned at her. "I'm not so sad about Bus Thirteen, though."

Just then, Bus Eleven pulled up.

Destiny climbed on.

The steps were clean and shiny.

The bus had blue seats and a rug on the floor.

She kept thinking about Ms. Katz.
What could they do?
Wait. She had an idea.
Was it a good one?
She wasn't an excellent thinker.
But she was trying.
Maybe it would work.

CHAPTER 6

TUESDAY

It was time for the Afternoon Center. Destiny started down the stairs. She passed the school-yard window.

Bus Thirteen was parked outside all by itself.

It didn't look so bad when it wasn't driving kids around.

Just a plain old bus.

Mrs. Terrible Thomas, the cat, was up on the roof.

She was having a sunbath.

The kittens were down below. They were climbing up the side of their box.

Destiny could see a little orange paw.

But there was no time to watch buses and kittens. Even though she loved that orange ice cat.

"Hurry," she told herself.

She rushed down the stairs.

She was almost flying.

It was a good thing Ms. Katz was still in the library. She wasn't so happy with kids flying down the stairs.

But saving Ms. Katz was more important than staying on the ground.

Yolanda was on the bottom step.

"I thought and thought," said Yolanda. "I have an idea."

"I thought and thought, too," said Destiny. "And I have an idea, too." She sank down on the step.

"First," Yolanda said, "we should tell the whole Afternoon Center about this."

"Tell Ms. Katz?"

Yolanda shook her head. "Not Ms. Katz. She'd be too sad. And not Jake, either."

"No, not Jake," Destiny said.

Destiny looked up at the ceiling. "Maybe it would be better not to tell the grown-ups yet."

She leaned forward.

She had to talk fast.

Jake would be coming down the hall with his broom any minute.

Destiny could see two ice cream cups, four smushed-up homework papers, and an ant just waiting to be swept up.

"My idea is we'll ask everyone to write poems," Destiny said. "Hundreds of poems. Thousands of poems. All about Ms. Katz."

"Millions," said Yolanda. She rubbed at her stained shirt.

It must have been through the wash, Destiny thought. She could see only a pale little spot.

Yolanda shook her head. "It's too bad I'm not a better poet."

"It's too bad I'm not a better reader," said Destiny.

"You don't have to read," Yolanda said. "You just have to make up the poems!"

Destiny took a breath. "Hey, I never thought of that."

They flew into the lunchroom.

Today the snack was fat pretzel rods. Four to a person.

Destiny counted them out.

She made a few mistakes.

"Hey," Gina said. "I have only three and a half pretzels."

Destiny whispered in her ear.

"Oh, no!" Gina said. "I'll start a poem as soon as I finish my snack. It won't take me long. I don't have as many pretzels as everyone else."

Destiny told Mitchell the news and Yolanda told Habib.

"Good thing you gave me six pretzels," Habib said. "I think better when my stomach is full."

Soon all the pretzels were given out.

Everyone knew about writing poems for Ms. Katz.

There were no pretzels left for Destiny.

That was all right.

She ate the salt at the bottom of the bag. Then she went outside with Yolanda.

Peter Petway was out there already. But he wasn't playing ball with Ramón.

He was working on the *Zigzag News—Read All About It.*

Destiny leaned up against the bricks of the school.

She pulled a piece of paper out of her pocket.

Yolanda pulled out paper, too. "Do you know what rhymes with Katz?" she asked.

"Hats," Destiny said.

"That's good," Yolanda said. "Ms. Katz has a great baseball hat."

Destiny could see her lips moving.

"Ah," Yolanda said. "How about this? *I like Ms. Katz. I like her hats.*"

Destiny nodded.

She thought of a poem. She wrote quickly.

Ms. Katz is the best.
She never gives tests.

Yolanda leaned over her shoulder. "You're turning out to be an excellent thinker."

Destiny closed her eyes.

Yes, she was feeling happy.

Not only was she an excellent thinker. She was going to save Ms. Katz.

She just knew it.

Orange Ice kitten climbed out of the box and tumbled to the ground.

Destiny stood up.

She raced over to the kitten and put her back in the box.

"There. Safe," Destiny said.

She patted the kitten's soft little head.

CHAPTER 7

WEDNESDAY

In the lunchroom, Destiny gave out pears. Mr. Oakley had brought in a basketful.

The pears had little brown spots. They had a few dents, too.

"Pears again?" said Mitchell. "I'm going to turn into a pear."

Destiny bit into one.

Yolanda was sitting at a table. She was drawing a picture of Ms. Katz.

Destiny knew that because it said *Ms. Katz* underneath.

Yolanda drew a gray kitten.

"That's Ms. Katz's favorite one," Yolanda said.

She drew eyeglasses on Ms. Katz . . . and on the cat, too.

"It's a little bit of a joke," she said. "On the top I'll write a poem. Something like: *Cats are sweet. Ms. Katz is . . .*"

"Neat," Destiny said.

"Yes!" Yolanda said.

Mitchell gave a little *shu-shu* whistle. "Great rhyming," he said. "Great picture."

Yolanda held up the picture.

But then she shook her head. "Too bad. There's a little pear goo on the edge."

Destiny held up her hands. There was pear goo on her fingers.

"There's some on my sneakers," said Mitchell.

"Mine too," Charlie said.

But they couldn't worry about that.

They had to hang up poems all over the Afternoon Center.

Everyone helped.

Destiny looked down the hall. "Some are a little crooked," she said.

"And there's pear goo on the floor," Mitchell said.

Jake came down the hall. He was sweeping his way along.

At the same time, Ramón blew his whistle.

Afternoon Center was over.

"Good thing," Mitchell said.

There was no time for Jake to scold them for the mess.

Everyone scrambled outside.

The walkers ran for the gate.

The busers ran for the buses.

Destiny climbed onto the bus. She sat next to the window.

She could see Bus Thirteen in back of the school yard.

Poor bus with nothing to do.

Then she saw something else.

Someone was coming.

It was Yolanda. She was running toward the bus.

She was waving at Destiny.

Waving hard.

Destiny leaned against the bus window. Too bad it was glued shut.

"Wait!" Yolanda called.

The bus didn't wait.

The driver honked the horn.
The bus began to pull out of the school yard.
Destiny looked back over her shoulder.
Charlie looked back, too.

Yolanda was yelling something.
"What is she saying?" Destiny asked.
Beebe was sitting right behind Destiny.

She tapped Destiny on the shoulder. "I can read lips sometimes," she said.

Destiny held her breath.

Beebe was smiling. "Yolanda said she had an idea. You can use Bus Thirteen to help Ms. Katz."

"But how?" Destiny asked.

CHAPTER 8

THURSDAY

Yolanda's new idea was super!

But first they had to find Jake.

Destiny and Yolanda looked out the door to the playground.

Beebe and Gina were running a race. The gray kitten was racing after them.

Clifton was hopping along the fence. A kitten was trying to climb it.

Ramón was playing basketball with Mitchell. And there was Jake in the middle of the yard, sweeping.

Destiny and Yolanda rushed outside.

"I'm crossing my fingers," Destiny said. "This has to work."

"I'm crossing my toes," said Yolanda.

Jake was waving his arms around. His face was red.

"He doesn't look happy," Destiny whispered to Yolanda.

"Something has to be done," Jake was muttering.

Destiny closed her eyes for a moment. Poor, poor Ms. Katz.

"Hi, Jake," she said.

"Hi, girls," Jake said back.

Destiny began. "Yolanda is an artist," she said.

"Nice," said Jake.

He began to sweep again.

Mrs. Terrible Thomas walked by. Her six kittens followed in a row.

Orange Ice was last.

"We could all fix up Bus Thirteen," Destiny said.

"That bus is finished!" Jake said. "I'm just trying to think of how to get rid of it."

"It would make a great place for Ms. Katz's poetry people," Yolanda said.

Jake squinted

at the bus. "Well . . . ," he began. "Maybe we could do that. We wouldn't have papers all over the wall. We might not have pear goo all over the floor."

"And Ms. Katz wouldn't take up so much room," Yolanda said. "You wouldn't have to get rid of her at all."

"What?" Jake said. "Get rid of . . ."

Destiny could hardly get the words out. "Get rid of Ms. Katz."

Jake opened his eyes wide. "Didn't you read the poems? They say what a great teacher Ms. Katz is."

Destiny looked at Yolanda.

The poems were working.

Destiny really *was* an excellent thinker. She bet no one even remembered that little rainbow/ rhyme mistake.

"No one wants to get rid of Ms. Katz," Jake said. He leaned on his broom. "She's the best teacher at the Zigzag School."

Wait a minute. *Something was strange here,* Destiny thought.

"I heard you . . . ," she began.

Yolanda spoke at the same time. "But Destiny said . . ."

"You said Ms. Katz had to go," they finished together.

Jake looked surprised.

Super surprised.

Then he began to laugh. "That's not it," he said. "Look around."

Destiny looked around.

She looked as hard as she could.

The handball court was right there.

Someone had dropped half a sandwich in front of it.

There were ball players and racers. There was a squirrel sitting in the tree.

Destiny put her hand up to her mouth.

"Do you see what I mean?" Jake said.

The striped kittens were growing up. They were racing up and down the steps.

The gray kitten was almost as big as Mrs. Terrible Thomas.

Two black and white kittens were climbing on the trash basket. They were tipping it over.

Even Orange Ice wasn't a tiny kitten anymore.

She was a cat.

"Cats!" Destiny said. "That's what you said."

"Not *Ms*. Katz!" Yolanda said.

Jake nodded. "We have to find homes for my cats."

There was a strange feeling in Destiny's chest.

A good feeling.

Ms. Katz would stay at the Zigzag School forever.

Then a bad feeling.

She'd made a terrible mistake. Again.

CHAPTER 9

FRIDAY

Destiny was giving out snacks. Today it was cheese sticks.

She tried not to look at anyone.

She knew what everybody thought.

They thought that Destiny Washington wasn't an excellent thinker.

She wasn't a thinker at all!

After snack, Gina said, "Come on. Let's go look at the bus."

They crossed the school yard.

Lots of grown-ups were there. Destiny's mother, Mitchell's father. Mr. Oakley. And Jake, of course.

Yolanda was inside Bus Thirteen. She hadn't stopped for a snack.

She was painting the windows.

She'd drawn a picture of Beebe and Sumiko. They were jumping rope.

There was another one of Mitchell and Charlie playing ball with Ramón.

There was one of Peter Petway. He was working on the *Zigzag News—Read All About It*.

There was a picture of Ms. Katz with her glasses. She was holding a gray cat.

Below, Yolanda had written *LOVELY!* in hot-pink letters.

It was Ms. Katz's favorite word.

Destiny stepped around to see the front of the bus.

A picture took up the whole window.

Angel said, "It's the best one."

Gina gave Destiny a poke. "It's you," she said. "And Yolanda."

Destiny swallowed. It really was the best painting.

Yolanda was on one side.

Destiny was on the other.

They were leaning toward each other.

And in the middle—

Destiny had to smile.

There was a flying chocolate pudding with a whipped cream hat.

And now, Yolanda was outside. She was writing something else under the picture.

"Don't look yet," she called out to Destiny.

Destiny turned around. She looked at the Zigzag School.

She looked at the sky and two small birds flying by.

She looked at the flag. It was blowing in the wind.

She wondered what Yolanda was writing.

Then Gina whispered something to Angel.

"What?" Destiny asked.

"Good thing I can read lips." Beebe leaned forward. She was watching Gina and Angel talk. "Yes, it's true about Destiny," she said.

"Turn around now!" Yolanda called.

Destiny turned.

Destiny's mom was leaning over Yolanda's shoulder. She was smiling.

Destiny could see the letters under Yolanda's picture.

Every letter was different.

One was purple.

One was orange.

One was green.

They were rainbow colors.

Destiny liked rainbows again.

She wasn't such a hot reader. But she could read these words.

They said:

Destiny Washington really tries.
She's going to get a super

Yolanda stopped. "I can't make this rhyme."

Destiny thought about it.

She made a million mistakes.

She wasn't such a great reader.

But it was true. She really did try.

Destiny could see that Yolanda was still thinking of a rhyme.

Destiny thought, too.

But there was only one word she could think of.

CHAPTER 10

STILL FRIDAY

Destiny climbed onto the bus.

Jake had worked hard.

He'd taken out some of the seats. He'd put in a skinny table.

He'd swept the floor.

Cats were running all over the place.

Up on the seats. Up on the table.

Mrs. Terrible Thomas was asleep in the driver's seat.

Destiny gave her mom a hug.

Mitchell shook his father's hand.

Destiny picked up Orange Ice Cat. She could hear her purr.

She was the cutest cat in the world.

Then everyone waited.

Jake had gone to get Ms. Katz.

Peter Petway was writing a story for the *Zigzag News—Read All About It.*

Beebe was tying a pink ribbon around the gray cat's neck.

Destiny looked out the bus window.

Now Jake and Ms. Katz were hurrying across the school yard.

"Surprise!" everyone yelled.

Ms. Katz looked around.

"It's the new poetry place," Destiny said.

"Lovely," Ms. Katz said. "Just lovely."

She looked at the gray kitten. "A pink ribbon," she said.

"The kitten is for you," Jake said.

Ms. Katz blinked. "That's another surprise."

"I'm taking a black and white cat," Peter Petway said. "She looks like a newspaper."

"A striped one for me," said Mitchell.

"Me too," said Charlie.

"I'm taking the other black and white one," Mr. Oakley said. "She'll love to climb my pear trees."

Destiny was still holding Orange Ice Cat.

Too bad. All she had were fourteen fish. They gulped in water. They flicked their tails.

"I was thinking," Destiny's mom said. "Orange is your favorite color."

"That's right," Yolanda said.

Destiny's mom nodded. "And fish aren't very exciting pets."

Destiny held Orange Ice Cat a little harder.

"Here's the rest of the poem," Yolanda said.

"Destiny really tries.
She's going to get a super surprise."

61

Destiny's mom nodded.

Destiny took a breath. Orange Ice Cat was going home with her!

Mitchell whistled. It was loud. It was piercing!

"Read all about it in the *Zigzag News*!" Peter Petway said.

Destiny nodded. Orange Ice Cat purred even louder.

It had been the best week at the Zigzag Afternoon Center.

PATRICIA REILLY GIFF is the author of many beloved books for children, including the Kids of the Polk Street School books, the Friends and Amigos books, and the Polka Dot Private Eye books. Several of her novels for older readers have been chosen as ALA-ALSC Notable Children's Books and ALA-YALSA Best Books for Young Adults. They include *The Gift of the Pirate Queen; All the Way Home; Water Street; Nory Ryan's Song,* a Society of Children's Book Writers and Illustrators Golden Kite Honor Book for Fiction; and the Newbery Honor Books *Lily's Crossing* and *Pictures of Hollis Woods. Lily's Crossing* was also chosen as a *Boston Globe–Horn Book* Honor Book. Her books for younger readers in the Zigzag Kids series are *Number One Kid, Big Whopper, Flying Feet, Star Time,* and *Bears Beware.* Her most recent books for older readers include *R My Name Is Rachel, Storyteller, Eleven,* and *Wild Girl.* Patricia Reilly Giff lives in Connecticut.

Patricia Reilly Giff is available for select readings and lectures. To inquire about a possible appearance, please contact the Random House Speakers Bureau at rhspeakers@randomhouse.com.

ALASDAIR BRIGHT is a freelance illustrator who has worked on numerous books and advertising projects. He loves drawing and is never without his sketchbook. He lives in Bedford, England.

More afternoon fun
for everyone at
the Zigzag School